SCHOOL STORIES

Your Dog Didn't Eat

SeaStar Books

NEW YORK

Special thanks to Leigh Ann Jones, Valerie Lewis, Walter Mayes, and Marian Reiner for the consultation services and invaluable support they provided for the creation of this book.

Reading Rainbow® is a production of GPN/Nebraska ETV and WNED-TV Buffalo and is produced by Lancit Media Entertainment, Ltd., a JuniorNet Company. *Reading Rainbow*® is a registered trademark of GPN/WNED-TV.

SeaStar Books · A division of North-South Books, Inc.

ISBN 1-58717-038-8 (library binding) 10 9 8 7 6 5 4 3 2 1
ISBN 1-58717-037-X (paperback) 10 9 8 7 6 5 4 3 2 1

Contents

The Circle

BY Jean Van Leeuwen

PICTURES BY Ann Schweninger

In Mrs. Flora Pig's room
there was so much to do,
Amanda didn't know what to do first.
She played in the dress-up corner.
"Look, Lollipop," she said.
"I'm a farmer astronaut."

She played in the make-believe corner.

"I can't believe it," she said.

"A whole suitcase full of puppets.

Hi, Mr. Rabbit. You should meet

my rabbit. Her name is Sallie."

She played in the building corner.
"I never saw so many blocks," she said.
"I'll make a skyscraper. Or a city.
Or maybe the whole world!"

Mrs. Flora Pig's room had giant ABC's
and a piano and boxes called cubbies.

"Cubbies?" said Amanda.
"What are those for?"
"For things you bring to school
and the work you take home,"
said Mrs. Flora Pig.

"I want to do a lot of work,"
said Amanda.

"Soon we will," said Mrs. Flora Pig.
"But right now we are going to sit
in a circle and get to know each other."

Amanda saw a circle of little chairs
and one big one.
The big one must be for me,
she thought,
because I am so big now.
Amanda sat in the big chair.

Mrs. Flora Pig sat next to her.
But something was wrong.
Her knees were next to her ears.

"That's the teacher's chair, silly,"
said a tiny boy.
"Oops," said Amanda.
She and the teacher changed chairs.

"Now we are going to play a game,"
said Mrs. Flora Pig.
"I call it the name game."
She pointed at herself.
"My name is Mrs. Flora Pig," she said.
"And I like to play the piano."
She pointed at the tiny boy.

"My name is William," said the boy.
"And I like big trucks."

She pointed at a girl dressed in pink.
"My name is Lily," said the girl.
"And I like my baby sister."

She pointed at Lollipop.
Lollipop didn't say anything.
Instead of her lollipop,
she was sucking her thumb.

"Why doesn't she talk?" asked William.
"She will talk when she is ready,"
said Mrs. Flora Pig.
"Maybe today. Maybe tomorrow."

She pointed at Amanda.

"My name is Amanda," said Amanda.
"And I like ballet and my new dress
and Sallie Rabbit and ice cream
and my brother Oliver and purple
and singing songs.

But the very best thing I like
is being a schoolgirl."

"How nice," said Mrs. Flora Pig.

Teach Us, Amelia Bedelia

BY Peggy Parish
PICTURES BY Lynn Sweat

Amelia Bedelia got her things.

She walked to school.

"Where is Mr. Carter's office?"

she asked.

"That first door," said a child.

Amelia Bedelia walked in.

"Mrs. Rogers tried to call you,"
she said. "But your telephone
is out of order."
"I know," said Mr. Carter.
"But thank goodness you're here.
The children are going wild.
Miss Lane left a list for today.
I'll take you to the room."
He handed Amelia Bedelia the list.

"Follow me," he said.

They went down the hall.

Mr. Carter opened a door.

Children were all over the place.

"All right," said Mr. Carter.

"Quiet! This is your new teacher."

"Me! Teach!" said Amelia Bedelia.

But Mr. Carter was gone.

She looked at the children.

They looked at her.

"I'm Amelia Bedelia," she said.

The children giggled.

She held up the list.
"We must do just what this says,"
she said. "Now, what's first?"

Amelia Bedelia read,
"'Call the roll.'"
She looked puzzled.
"Call the roll! What roll?"
she said.

"Does anybody have a roll?"

"I have," said Peter.

"Do get it," said Amelia Bedelia.

Peter opened his lunch box.

"Here it is," he said.

"Now I have to call it,"
said Amelia Bedelia.
"Roll! Hey, roll!
All right, that takes care of that."
The children roared.

Amelia Bedelia read her list.

She said, "It's science time.

Each of you should plant a bulb.

Do you know about that?"

"Yes," said Tim.

"We brought our pots."

"Where are the bulbs?"
said Amelia Bedelia.
"In the top closet," said Rebecca.
"Miss Lane said so."
Amelia Bedelia looked and looked.
"Nothing here but some
dried-up onions," she said.

"You all go outside.

Put some soil in your pots.

I'll go buy some bulbs."

Amelia Bedelia went to the store.

She hurried back.

The children were waiting.

"Here's a bulb for you and you,"
said Amelia Bedelia.
She gave everybody a bulb.
The children looked surprised.
Then they started giggling.
But they planted those bulbs.
They put the pots on the window sill.

"Those do look right pretty,"
said Amelia Bedelia.
"And I learned something new.
I didn't know you could plant bulbs."
Suddenly a bell rang.
"What's that for?"
said Amelia Bedelia.
"Free time," yelled the children.
"Good," said Amelia Bedelia.

Sparky and Eddie: The First Day of School

BY Tony Johnston

PICTURES BY Susannah Ryan

Sparky was tall.
Eddie was short.
Sparky had freckles.
Eddie had none.
Sparky liked trees.
Eddie liked bugs.
They were so different,
they were best friends.

Sparky and Eddie wanted
to start school.
They wanted to be
in the same room, too.
Their parents took them
to school one day to see
who their teachers would be.
The room lists were up.

Sparky would have Mr. Lopez.

Eddie would have Ms. Bean.

Sparky and Eddie looked at each other.

They gasped,

"We're not in the same room!"

They felt glum.

Too glum to even cry.

It was the first day of school.
Eddie went to his room.
Ms. Bean was waiting, smiling.

She had a rhinoceros beetle on her desk.

Eddie thought it was beautiful.

Ms. Bean let the kids look at it.

She let the kids touch it.

Some kids said, "Oooh!"

Some kids said, "Aaah!"

Eddie said, "*OOOH!*" and "*AAAH!*"

Sparky went to his room.

Mr. Lopez was waiting, smiling.

He had a bonsai on his desk.

The bonsai was short.

A dwarf, really. A dwarf tree.

Mr. Lopez let the kids look at it.

He let the kids touch it.

Some kids said, "Oooh!"

Some kids said, "Aaah!"

Sparky said, "*OOOH!*"

and "*AAAH!*"

Sparky and Eddie met
at the boys' bathroom.
"Do you like your teacher?" asked Eddie.
"Yes," said Sparky.
"He has a bonsai on his desk."

"What's that?" Eddie asked.

"A short tree."

"Short like me?"

"Shorter."

"COOL!" Eddie said.

"Do you like your teacher?"
asked Sparky.

"Yes," said Eddie.

"She has a rhinoceros beetle on her desk."

"WOW!" Sparky yelled.

"*A rhinoceros on her desk!*"

"It's a beetle," said Eddie.

Then he said,

"School is fun. I will stay.

I can be your best friend,

even if we're not in the same room."

"Me, too," said Sparky.

SCHOOL

BY Jean Little

PICTURES BY Jennifer Plecas

On Monday, Sally read first.

"Very good, Sally," Mr. Kent said.

"Now it is your turn, Emma."

Emma hung her head and whispered.

"Try to speak up, Emma,"

said Mr. Kent.

The recess bell rang.

"Emma can read after recess,"

Mr. Kent said.

Sally and Emma went outside.

"I wish I could read like you,"
Emma said.

"Emma, I heard you read to Josh.
You are a good reader," Sally said.

Emma looked down.

"Reading to Josh is easy," she said.

"Reading at school is not."

"Why not?" asked Sally.

"When they all look at me,

I try to speak up," said Emma.

"But only a whisper comes out."

Sally looked at Emma for a minute.

"I have an idea," she said.

"When we go in, keep your boots on.

Say, 'Magic Boots, make me brave.

Make me a good reader.'"

"It won't help," said Emma.

"It can't hurt to try," Sally said.

Emma kept her boots on.
Mr. Kent gave her the book.

Emma stood tall.
"Magic Boots, help," she whispered.

Then she began to read.

She read in a loud, clear voice.

"Good for you," said Mr. Kent.

"Way to go, Emma!" Sally said.

"Your magic boots did it."

"With the help of my magic friend,"
said Emma.

Be My Valentine

BY Amy Ehrlich

PICTURES BY Steven Kellogg

Leo, Zack, and Emmie were
shopping in the five-and-ten.
They went up one row
and down another
until they came to a row
of valentine cards.

"Oh, goody!" said Emmie.
"Valentine's Day is my
favorite holiday."
"I think it stinks," said Zack.
"Only girls like Valentine's Day."

"I'm a boy and I like it," said Leo.
"You would," said Zack.

They got to the checkout line.
Emmie had picked out
pink hearts, red lace paper,
and gold and silver markers.
"Come over to my house," she said.
"We'll make our own valentine cards."
"Not me," said Zack. "Forget it."
He turned right
and Leo and Emmie turned left.

At Emmie's house
they spread everything out
on the kitchen table.
Then they drew and cut and pasted
all afternoon.

"I'm making cards
for the girls in our class
but not for the boys," said Emmie.

"I'm making cards for everyone,"
said Leo.
His cards were messier than Emmie's
but they were bigger too.
Leo was very proud of them.

On Valentine's Day
he got to school early
and sneaked into Miss Davis's class.

It was so early that it was still dark.

Leo left a valentine card
on each person's desk.

Then he went home for breakfast.

In the playground
before school started,
everyone was telling secrets
about Valentine's Day.
Some of the girls
kept pointing at Zack
and giggling.

"What's so funny?" Zack asked.
But they just giggled more
and ran away.
"I don't get it," said Zack.
"Those girls like you," said Emmie.
"You'll see."

Sure enough,
when they got to Miss Davis's room,
Zack's desk was piled high
with valentine cards.

Everyone else had at least one card
because Leo had made a card
for everyone.
But Leo didn't have any.

He tried not to feel bad.

It had been fun making the cards.

That's why he had done it.

After school Zack and Emmie
caught up with Leo.
"I'm sorry I didn't give you a card,"
said Emmie.
"All the ones I got were dumb,"
said Zack. "Yours was the best."

Leo stopped walking.
"You two are my friends, right?"
he asked.

"Right!" said Zack and Emmie.

"Okay," said Leo.

"Then I have one more question.
Will you be my valentine?"

"Sure!" Emmie said, giving him a hug.

"Valentine's Day is for girls,"
said Zack.

"Here we go again!" said Emmie.